A Note to Parents and Caregivers:

Read-it! Joke Books are for children who are moving ahead on the amazing road to reading. These fun books support the acquisition and extension of reading skills as well as a love of books.

Published by the same company that produces *Read-it!* Readers, these books introduce the question/answer and dialogue patterns that help children expand their thinking about language structure and book formats.

When sharing joke books with a child, read in short stretches. Pause often to talk about the pictures and the meaning of the jokes. The question/answer and dialogue formats work well for this purpose. Have the child turn the pages and point to the pictures and familiar words. When you read the jokes, have fun creating the voices of characters or emphasizing some important words. And be sure to reread favorite jokes.

There is no right or wrong way to share books with children. Find time to read with your child, and pass on the legacy of literacy.

Adria F. Klein, Ph.D.
Professor Emeritus
California State University
San Bernardino, California

Managing Editor: Bob Temple
Creative Director: Terri Foley
Editor: Peggy Henrikson
Editorial Adviser: Andrea Cascardi
Designer: Amy Muehlenhardt
Page production: Picture Window Books
The illustrations in this book were prepared digitally.

Picture Window Books
5115 Excelsior Boulevard
Suite 232
Minneapolis, MN 55416
1-877-845-8392
www.picturewindowbooks.com

Printed in the United States of America.

Library of Congress Cataloging-in-Publication Data
Dahl, Michael.
Doctor, doctor / written by Michael Dahl ; illustrated by Brian Jensen.
p. cm.— (Read-it! joke books)
Summary: A collection of jokes about doctors and patients, including,
"Patient: 'Doctor, doctor, my sister thinks she's an elevator.' Doctor:
'Send her right up.'"
ISBN 1-4048-0305-X
1. Medicine—Juvenile humor. 2. Wit and humor, Juvenile. [1. Medicine—
Wit and humor. 2. Jokes.] I. Jensen, Brian, ill. II. Title.
PN6231.M4 D26 2004
818'.5402—dc22
                                                              2003016666

Doctor, Doctor

A Book of Doctor Jokes

Read-it! Joke Books
Green Level

Michael Dahl • Illustrated by Brian Jensen

Reading Advisers:
Adria F. Klein, Ph.D.
Professor Emeritus, California State University
San Bernardino, California

Susan Kesselring, M.A., Literacy Educator
Rosemount-Apple Valley-Eagan (Minnesota) School District

PICTURE WINDOW BOOKS
Minneapolis, Minnesota

Patient: "Doctor, doctor, my brother is invisible!"

Doctor: "Sorry, but I can't see him."   5

Patient: "Doctor, doctor, my sister thinks she's an elevator."

Doctor: "Send her right up."

Patient: "Doctor, doctor, my nose keeps running."

Doctor: "Wait for it to get tired. You'll be able to catch it."

Patient: "Doctor, doctor, I need glasses."

Salesperson: "You sure do!
This is a shoe store."

Patient: "Doctor, doctor, I feel like a deck of cards."

Doctor: "I'll deal with you later."

Patient: "Doctor, doctor,
I think I'm a bridge.
What's come over me?"

Doctor: "Three cars, a truck, and a motorcycle." 13

Patient: "Doctor, doctor, I seem to be shrinking!"

Doctor: "Sorry, but you'll just
have to be a little patient."

Patient: "Doctor, doctor,
I think I'm a dog."
Doctor: "How long have you
felt this way?"

Patient: "Ever since
I was a puppy."

Patient: "Doctor, doctor,
I feel like a pair of curtains."

Doctor: "Please, pull
yourself together."

17

Patient: "Doctor, doctor, I feel like a spider."

Doctor: "Don't worry.
You've just caught a bug."

Patient: "Doctor, doctor, I just swallowed a roll of film."

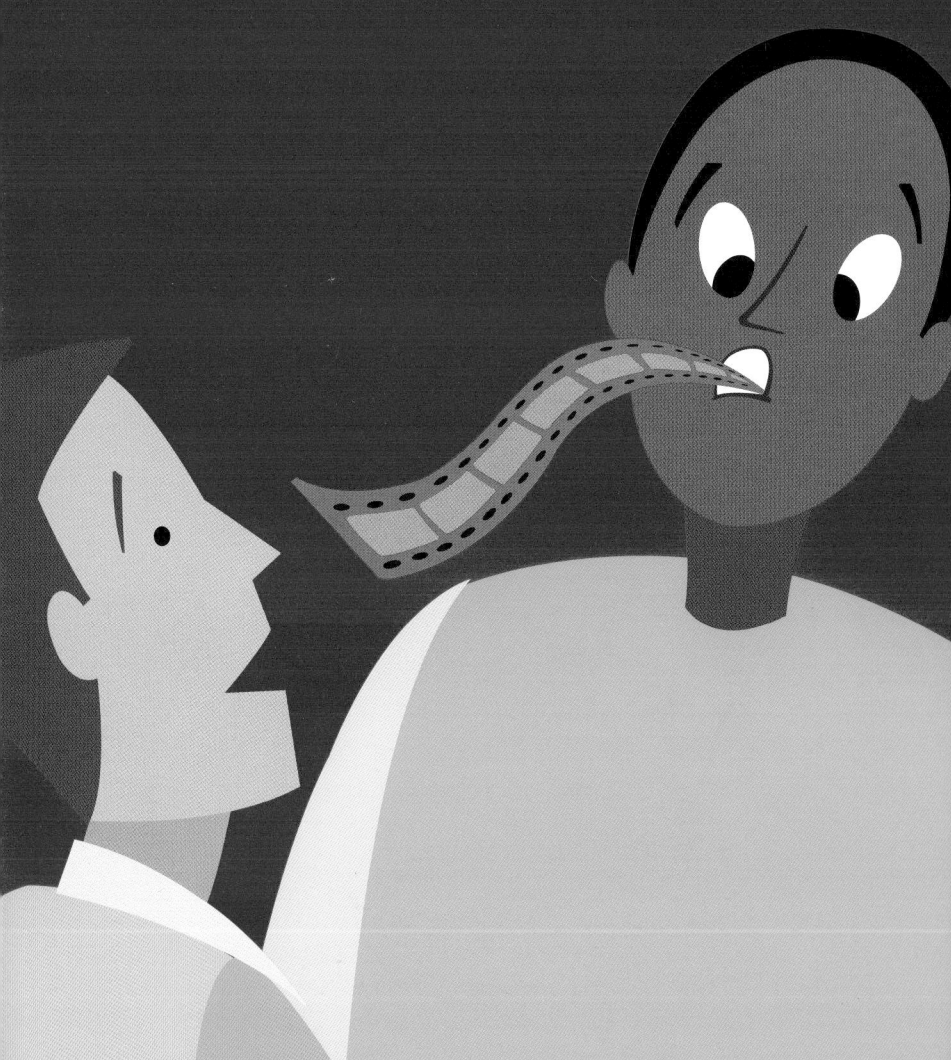

Doctor: "Let's see what develops."

Patient: "Doctor, doctor, my sister just swallowed my pencil."

Doctor: "Then use a pen."

Patient: "Doctor, doctor, I think I'm an electric eel."

Doctor: "How shocking!"

Patient: "Doctor, doctor, I think I'm turning into a thumbtack."

Doctor: "I see your point!"